' "She's an adventuress. Yes, an adventuress, but an end-of-the-century one. She doesn't travel for profit, but for pleasure." '

THE YELLOW BOOK
1894–1897

In early 1894, the first volume of *The Yellow Book* appeared and was a runaway success with readers. Disaster struck, however, in April 1895, when Oscar Wilde was arrested whilst supposedly carrying a copy of the magazine under his arm (in fact it was an entirely different book). *The Yellow Book* became a byword for decadence and immorality; the publisher's offices were attacked; authors protested; its art editor Aubrey Beardsley was sacked. Rising above this adverse publicity, the magazine continued until April 1897, when its thirteenth and final volume appeared. Despite its varied output – with entries by writers and illustrators both conservative and radical, famous and unknown, male and female – it has ever since been associated with decadence, aestheticism and the heady, avant-garde 'yellow nineties'.

The Yellow Book

PENGUIN BOOKS

PENGUIN CLASSICS

UK | USA | Canada | Ireland | Australia
India | New Zealand | South Africa

Penguin Classics is part of the Penguin Random House group of companies
whose addresses can be found at global.penguinrandomhouse.com.

This selection first published in Penguin Classics 2016
001

Set in 9.5/13 pt Baskerville 10 Pro
Typeset by Jouve (UK), Milton Keynes
Printed in Great Britain by Clays Ltd, St Ives plc

A CIP catalogue record for this book is available from the British Library

ISBN: 978-0-241-25222-2

www.greenpenguin.co.uk

MIX
Paper from
responsible sources
FSC® C018179

Penguin Random House is committed to a
sustainable future for our business, our readers
and our planet. This book is made from Forest
Stewardship Council® certified paper.

Contents

Announcement, March 1894

The aim of the Publishers and Editors of THE YELLOW BOOK is to depart as far as may be from the bad old traditions of periodical literature, and to provide an Illustrated Magazine which shall be beautiful as a piece of bookmaking, modern and distinguished in its letter-press and its pictures, and withal popular in the better sense of the word.

Altogether, it is expected that THE YELLOW BOOK will prove the most interesting, unusual, and important publication of its kind that has ever been undertaken. It will be charming, it will be daring, it will be distinguished. It will be a *book* – a book to be read, and placed upon one's shelves, and read again; a book in form, a book in substance; a book beautiful to see and convenient to handle; a book with style, a book with finish; a book that every book-lover will love at first sight; a book that will make book-lovers of many who are now indifferent to books.

La Dame aux Camélias

Suggestion

By Mrs Ernest Leverson

If Lady Winthrop had not spoken of me as 'that intolerable, effeminate boy,' she might have had some chance of marrying my father. She was a middle-aged widow; prosaic, fond of domineering, and an alarmingly excellent housekeeper; the serious work of her life was paying visits; in her lighter moments she collected autographs. She was highly suitable and altogether insupportable; and this unfortunate remark about me was, as people say, the last straw. Some encouragement from father Lady Winthrop must, I think, have received; for she took to calling at odd hours, asking my sister Marjorie sudden abrupt questions, and being generally impossible. A tradition existed that her advice was of use to our father in his household, and when, last year, he married his daughter's school-friend, a beautiful girl of twenty, it surprised every one except Marjorie and myself.

The whole thing was done, in fact, by suggestion. I shall never forget that summer evening when father first realised, with regard to Laura Egerton, the possible. He was

3

giving a little dinner of eighteen people. *Through a mistake of Marjorie's* (my idea) Lady Winthrop did not receive her invitation till the very last minute. Of course she accepted – we knew she would – but unknowing that it was a dinner party, she came without putting on evening-dress.

Nothing could be more trying to the average woman than such a *contretemps;* and Lady Winthrop was not one to rise, sublimely, and laughing, above the situation. I can see her now, in a plaid blouse and a vile temper, displaying herself, mentally and physically, to the utmost disadvantage, while Marjorie apologised the whole evening, in pale blue crèpe-de-chine; and Laura, in yellow, with mauve orchids, sat – an adorable contrast – on my father's other side, with a slightly conscious air that was perfectly fascinating. It is quite extraordinary what trifles have their little effect in these matters. *I* had sent Laura the orchids, anonymously; I could not help it if she chose to think they were from my father. Also, I had hinted of his secret affection for her, and lent her Verlaine. I said I had found it in his study, turned down at her favourite page. Laura has, like myself, the artistic temperament; she is cultured, rather romantic, and in search of the *au-delà*. My father has at times – never to me – rather charming manners; also he is still handsome, with that look of having suffered that comes from enjoying oneself too much. That evening his really sham melancholy and apparently hollow gaiety were delightful for a son to witness, and appealed evidently to her heart. Yes, strange as it may seem, while the world said that pretty Miss Egerton married old Carington for his money, she was really in love, or thought herself in love, with our father. Poor girl! She little knew what an irritating, ill-tempered, absent-minded person he is in private life; and at times I have pangs of remorse.

A fortnight after the wedding, father forgot he was married, and began again treating Laura with a sort of *distrait* gallantry as Marjorie's friend, or else ignoring her altogether. When, from time to time, he remembers she is his wife, he scolds her about the housekeeping in a fitful, perfunctory way, for he does not know that Marjorie does it still. Laura bears the rebukes like an angel; indeed, rather than take the slightest practical trouble she would prefer to listen to the strongest language in my father's vocabulary.

But she is sensitive; and when father, speedily resuming his bachelor manners, recommenced his visits to an old friend who lives in one of the little houses opposite the Oratory, she seemed quite vexed. Father is horribly careless, and Laura found a letter. They had a rather serious explanation, and for a little time after, Laura seemed depressed. She soon tried to rouse herself, and is at times cheerful enough with Marjorie and myself, but I fear she has had a disillusion. They never quarrel now, and I think we all three dislike father about equally, though Laura never owns it, and is gracefully attentive to him in a gentle, filial sort of way.

5

We are fond of going to parties – not father – and Laura is a very nice chaperone for Marjorie. They are both perfectly devoted to me. 'Cecil knows everything,' they are always saying, and they do nothing – not even choosing a hat – without asking my advice.

Since I left Eton I am supposed to be reading with a tutor, but as a matter of fact I have plenty of leisure; and am very glad to be of use to the girls, of whom I'm, by the way, quite proud. They are rather a sweet contrast; Marjorie has the sort of fresh rosy prettiness you see in the park and on the river. She is tall, and slim as a punt-pole, and if she were not very careful how she dresses, she would look like a drawing by Pilotelle in the *Lady's Pictorial*. She is practical and lively, she rides and drives and dances; skates, and goes to some mysterious haunt called *The Stores*, and is, in her own way, quite a modern English type.

Laura has that exotic beauty so much admired by Philistines; dreamy dark eyes, and a wonderful white complexion. She loves music and poetry and pictures and admiration in a lofty sort of way; she has a morbid fondness for mental gymnastics, and a dislike to physical exertion, and never takes any exercise except waving her hair. Sometimes she looks bored, and I have heard her sigh.

'Cissy,' Marjorie said, coming one day into my study, 'I want to speak to you about Laura.'

'Do you have pangs of conscience too?' I asked, lighting a cigarette.

'Dear, we took a great responsibility. Poor girl! Oh, couldn't we make Papa more—'

'Impossible,' I said; 'no one has any influence with him. He can't bear even me, though if he had a shade of decency he would dash away an unbidden tear every time I look at him with my mother's blue eyes.'

My poor mother was a great beauty, and I am supposed to be her living image.

'Laura has no object in life,' said Marjorie. 'I have, all girls have, I suppose. By the way, Cissy, I am quite sure Charlie Winthrop is serious.'

'How sweet of him! I am so glad. I got father off my hands last season.'

'Must I really marry him, Cissy? He bores me.'

'What has that to do with it? Certainly you must. You are not a beauty, and I doubt your ever having a better chance.'

Marjorie rose and looked at herself in the long pier-glass that stands opposite my writing-table. I could not resist the temptation to go and stand beside her.

'I am just the style that is admired now,' said Marjorie, dispassionately.

'So am I,' I said reflectively. 'But *you* will soon be out of date.'

Every one says I am strangely like my mother. Her face was of that pure and perfect oval one so seldom sees, with delicate features, rosebud mouth, and soft flaxen hair. A blondness without insipidity, for the dark-blue eyes are fringed with dark lashes, and from their languorous depths looks out a soft mockery. I have a curious ideal devotion to my mother; she died when I was quite young – only two months old – and I often spend hours thinking of her, as I gaze at myself in the mirror.

'Do come down from the clouds,' said Marjorie impatiently, for I had sunk into a reverie. 'I came to ask you to think of something to amuse Laura – to interest her.'

'We ought to make it up to her in some way. Haven't you tried anything?'

'Only palmistry; and Mrs Wilkinson prophesied her all that she detests, and depressed her dreadfully.'

'What do you think she really needs most?' I asked.

Our eyes met.

'Really, Cissy, you're too disgraceful,' said Marjorie. There was a pause.

'And so I'm to accept Charlie?'

'What man do you like better?' I asked.

'I don't know what you mean,' said Marjorie, colouring.

'*I* thought Adrian Grant would have been more sympathetic to Laura than to you. I have just had a note from him, asking me to tea at his studio to-day.' I threw it to her. 'He says I'm to bring you both. Would that amuse Laura?'

'Oh,' cried Marjorie, enchanted, 'of course we'll go. I wonder what he thinks of me,' she added wistfully.

'He didn't say. He is going to send Laura his verses, "Heartsease and Heliotrope."'

She sighed. Then she said, 'Father was complaining again to-day of your laziness.'

'I, lazy! Why, I've been swinging the censer in Laura's boudoir because she wants to encourage the religious temperament, and I've designed your dress for the Clives' fancy ball.'

'Where's the design?'

'In my head. You're not to wear white; Miss Clive must wear white.'

'I wonder you don't marry her,' said Marjorie, 'you admire her so much.'

'I never marry. Besides, I know she's pretty, but that furtive Slade-school manner of hers gets on my nerves. You don't know how dreadfully I suffer from my nerves.'

She lingered a little, asking me what I advised her to choose for a birthday present for herself – an American organ, a black poodle, or an *édition de luxe* of Browning. I advised the last, as being least noisy. Then I told her I felt sure that in spite of her admiration for Adrian, she was far too good-natured to interfere with Laura's prospects. She said I was incorrigible, and left the room with a smile of resignation.

And I returned to my reading. On my last birthday – I was seventeen – my father – who has his gleams of dry humour – gave me *Robinson Crusoe*! I prefer Pierre Loti, and intend to have an onyx-paved bath-room, with soft apricot-coloured light shimmering through the blue-lined

9

green curtains in my chambers, as soon as I get Margorie married, and Laura more – settled down.

I met Adrian Grant first at a luncheon party at the Clives'. I seemed to amuse him; he came to see me, and became at once obviously enamoured of my step-mother. He is rather an impressionable impressionist, and a delightful creature, tall and graceful and beautiful, and altogether most interesting. Every one admits he's fascinating; he is very popular and very much disliked. He is by way of being a painter; he has a little money of his own – enough for his telegrams, but not enough for his button-holes – and nothing could be more incongruous than the idea of his marrying. I have never seen Marjorie so much attracted. But she is a good loyal girl, and will accept Charlie Winthrop, who is a dear person, good-natured and ridiculously rich – just the sort of man for a brother-in-law. It will annoy my old enemy Lady Winthrop – he is her nephew, and she wants him to marry that little Miss Clive. Dorothy Clive has her failings, but she could not – to do her justice – be happy with Charlie Winthrop.

Adrian's gorgeous studio gives one the complex impression of being at once the calm retreat of a mediæval saint and the luxurious abode of a modern Pagan. One feels that everything could be done there, everything from praying to flirting – everything except painting. The tea-party amused me, I was pretending to listen to a brown person who was talking absurd worn-out literary clichés – as that the New Humour is not funny, or that

Bourget understood women, when I overheard this fragment of conversation.

'But don't you like Society?' Adrian was saying.

'I get rather tired of it. People are so much alike. They all say the same things,' said Laura.

'Of course they all say the same things to *you*,' murmured Adrian, as he affected to point out a rather curious old silver crucifix.

'That,' said Laura, 'is one of the things they say.'

About three weeks later I found myself dining alone with Adrian Grant, at one of the two restaurants in London. (The cooking is better at the other, this one is the more becoming.) I had lilies-of-the-valley in my button-hole, Adrian was wearing a red carnation. Several people glanced at us. Of course he is very well known in Society. Also, I was looking rather nice, and I could not help hoping, while Adrian gazed rather absently over my head, that the shaded candles were staining to a richer rose the waking wonder of my face.

Adrian was charming of course, but he seemed worried and a little preoccupied, and drank a good deal of champagne.

Towards the end of dinner, he said – almost abruptly for him – 'Carington.'

'Cecil,' I interrupted. He smiled.

'Cissy . . . it seems an odd thing to say to you, but though you are so young, I think you know everything.

11

I am sure you know everything. You know about me. I am in love. I am quite miserable. What on earth am I to do!' He drank more champagne. 'Tell me,' he said, 'what to do.' For a few minutes, while we listened to that interminable hackneyed *Intermezzo*, I reflected; asking myself by what strange phases I had risen to the extraordinary position of giving advice to Adrian on such a subject?

Laura was not happy with our father. From a selfish motive, Marjorie and I had practically arranged that monstrous marriage. That very day he had been disagreeable, asking me with a clumsy sarcasm to raise his allowance, so that he could afford my favourite cigarettes. If Adrian were free, Marjorie might refuse Charlie Winthrop. I don't want her to refuse him. Adrian has treated me as a friend. I like him – I like him enormously. I am quite devoted to him. And how can I rid myself of the feeling of responsibility, the sense that I owe some compensation to poor beautiful Laura?

We spoke of various matters. Just before we left the table, I said, with what seemed, but was not, irrelevance, 'Dear Adrian, Mrs Carington—'

'Go on, Cissy.'

'She is one of those who must be appealed to, at first, by her imagination. She married our father because she thought he was lonely and misunderstood.'

'*I* am lonely and misunderstood,' said Adrian, his eyes flashing with delight.

'Ah, not twice! She doesn't like that now.'

I finished my coffee slowly, and then I said,

'Go to the Clives' fancy-ball as Tristan.'

Adrian pressed my hand . . .

At the door of the restaurant we parted, and I drove home through the cool April night, wondering, wondering. Suddenly I thought of my mother – my beautiful sainted mother, who would have loved me, I am convinced, had she lived, with an extraordinary devotion. What would she have said to all this? What would she have thought? I know not why, but a mad reaction seized me. I felt recklessly conscientious. My father! After all, he was my father. I was possessed by passionate scruples. If I went back now to Adrian – if I went back and implored him, supplicated him never to see Laura again!

I felt I could persuade him. I have sufficient personal magnetism to do that, if I make up my mind. After one glance in the looking-glass, I put up my stick and stopped the hansom. I had taken a resolution. I told the man to drive to Adrian's rooms.

He turned round with a sharp jerk. In another second a brougham passed us – a swift little brougham that I knew. It slackened – it stopped – we passed it – I saw my father. He was getting out at one of the little houses opposite the Brompton Oratory.

'Turn round again,' I shouted to the cabman. And he drove me straight home.

Night Piece

Stella Maris

By Arthur Symons

Why is it I remember yet
You, of all women one has met
In random wayfare, as one meets
The chance romances of the streets,
The Juliet of a night? I know
Your heart holds many a Romeo.
And I, who call to mind your face
In so serene a pausing-place,
Where the bright pure expanse of sea,
The shadowy shore's austerity,
Seems a reproach to you and me,
I too have sought on many a breast
The ecstasy of love's unrest,
I too have had my dreams, and met
(Ah me!) how many a Juliet.
Why is it, then, that I recall
You, neither first nor last of all?
For, surely as I see to-night
The glancing of the lighthouse light,
Against the sky, across the bay,
As turn by turn it falls my way,
So surely do I see your eyes

Out of the empty night arise,
Child, you arise and smile to me
Out of the night, out of the sea,
The Nereid of a moment there,
And is it seaweed in your hair?

O lost and wrecked, how long ago,
Out of the drowned past, I know,
You come to call me, come to claim
My share of your delicious shame.
Child, I remember, and can tell
One night we loved each other well;
And one night's love, at least or most,
Is not so small a thing to boast.
You were adorable, and I
Adored you to infinity,
That nuptial night too briefly borne
To the oblivion of morn.
Oh, no oblivion! for I feel
Your lips deliriously steal
Along my neck, and fasten there;
I feel the perfume of your hair,
And your soft breast that heaves and dips,
Desiring my desirous lips,
And that ineffable delight
When souls turn bodies, and unite
In the intolerable, the whole
Rapture of the embodied soul.

That joy was ours, we passed it by;
You have forgotten me, and I
Remember you thus strangely, won
An instant from oblivion.
And I, remembering, would declare
That joy, not shame, is ours to share,
Joy that we had the will and power,
In spite of fate, to snatch one hour,
Out of vague nights, and days at strife,
So infinitely full of life.
And 'tis for this I see you rise,
A wraith, with starlight in your eyes,
Here, where the drowsy-minded mood
Is one with Nature's solitude;
For this, for this, you come to me
Out of the night, out of the sea.

Garçons de Café

A Journey of Little Profit

By John Buchan

'The Devil he sang, the Devil he played
High and fast and free.
And this was ever the song he made,
As it was told to me.
"Oh, I am the king of the air and the ground,
And lord of the seasons' roll,
And I will give you a hundred pound,
If you will give me your soul."'

The Ballad of Grey Weather.

The cattle market of Inverforth is, as all men know north
of the Tweed, the greatest market of the kind in the land.
For days in the late Autumn there is the lowing of oxen
and the bleating of sheep among its high wooden pens,
and in the rickety sale-rings the loud clamour of auction-
eers and the talk of farmers. In the open yard where are
the drovers and the butchers, a race always ungodly and
law-despising, there is such a Babel of cries and curses

as might wake the Seven Sleepers. From twenty different adjacent eating-houses comes the clatter of knives, where the country folk eat their dinner of beef and potatoes, with beer for sauce, and the collies grovel on the ground for stray morsels. Hither come a hundred types of men from the Highland cateran with scarce a word of English, and the shentleman-farmer of Inverness and Ross, to lowland graziers and city tradesmen, not to speak of blackguards of many nationalities and more professions.

It was there I first met Duncan Stewart of Clachamharstan, in the Moor of Rannoch, and there I heard this story. He was an old man when I knew him, grizzled and wind-beaten; a prosperous man, too, with many herds like Jacob and much pasture. He had come down from the North with kyloes, and as he waited on the Englishmen with whom he had trysted, he sat with me through the long day and beguiled the time with many stories. He had been a drover in his youth, and had travelled on foot the length and breadth of Scotland; and his memory went back hale and vigorous to times which are now all but historical. This tale I heard among many others as we sat on a pen amid the smell of beasts and the jabber of Gaelic:

'When I was just turned of twenty-five I was a wild young lad as ever was heard of. I had taken to the droving for the love of a wild life, and a wild life I led. My father's heart would be broken long syne with my doings, and well for my mother that she was in her grave since I was six years old. I paid no heed to the ministrations of godly Mr Macdougall of the Isles, who bade me turn from the error of my ways, but went on my own evil course, making siller, for I was a braw lad at the work and a trusted, and knowing the inside of every public from the pier of Cromarty to the streets of York. I was a wild drinker, caring in my cups for neither God nor man, a great hand with the cards, and fond of the lassies past all telling. It makes me shameful to this day to think on my evil life when I was twenty-five.

'Well, it chanced that in the back of the month of September I found myself in the city of Edinburgh with a flock of fifty sheep which I had bought as a venture from a drunken bonnet-laird and was thinking of selling somewhere wast the country. They were braw beasts, Leicester every one of them, well-fed and dirt-cheap at the price I gave. So it was with a light heart that I drove them out of the town by the Merchiston Road along by the face of the Pentlands. Two or three friends came with me, all like myself for folly, but maybe a little bit poorer. Indeed, I cared little for them, and they valued me only for the whisky which I gave them to drink my health in at the parting. They left me on the near side of Colinton, and I went on my way alone.

'Now, if you'll be remembering the road, you will mind that at the place called Kirk Newton, just afore the road begins to twine over the Big Muir and almost at the head of the Water o' Leith, there is a verra fine public. Indeed, it would be no lee to call it the best public between Embro' and Glesca. The good wife, Lucky Craik by name, was an old friend of mine, for many a good gill of her prandy have I bought; so what would I be doing but just turning aside for refreshment? She met me at the door, verra pleased-like to see me, and soon I had my legs aneath her table and a basin of toddy on the board before me. And whom did I find in the same place but my old comrade Toshie Maclean from the backside of Glen-Lyon. Toshie and I were acquaintances so old that it did not behoove us to be parting quick. Forbye the day was chill without; and within the fire was grand and the crack of the best.

'Then Toshie and I got on quarrelling about the price of Lachlan Farawa's beasts that he sold at Falkirk; and, the drink having aye a bad effect on my temper, I was for giving him the lie and coming off in a great rage. It was about six o'clock in the evening and an hour to nightfall, so Mistress Craik comes in to try and keep me. "Losh, Duncan," says she, "ye'll never try and win ower the muir the nicht. It's mae than ten mile to Carnwath, and there's nocht atween it and this but whaups and heathery braes." But when I am roused I will be more obstinate than ten mules, so I would be going, though I knew not under Heaven where I was going till. I was too full of good liquor and good meat to be much worth at thinking, so I got my sheep on the road an a big bottle in my pouch and set off into the heather. I knew not what my purpose was, whether I thought to reach the shieling of Carnwath, or whether I expected some house of entertainment to spring up by the wayside. But my fool's mind was set on my purpose of getting some miles further in my journey ere the coming of darkness.

'For some time I jogged happily on, with my sheep running well before me and my dogs trotting at my heels. We left the trees behind and struck out on the broad grassy path which bands the moor like the waist-strap of a sword. It was most dreary and lonesome with never a house in view, only bogs and grey hillsides and ill-looking waters. It was stony, too, and this more than aught else caused my Dutch courage to fail me, for I soon fell wearied, since much whisky is bad travelling fare, and began to curse my folly. Had my pride no kept me back, I would have returned to Lucky Craik's; but I was like the devil for stiff-neckedness and thought of nothing but to push on.

'I own that I was verra well tired and quite spiritless when I first saw the House. I had scarce been an hour on the way, and the light was not quite gone; but still it was geyan dark, and the place sprang somewhat suddenly on my sight. For, looking a little to the left, I saw over a little strip of grass a big square dwelling with many outhouses, half farm and half pleasure-house. This, I thought, is the verra place I have been seeking and made sure of finding; so whistling a gay tune, I drove my flock toward it.

'When I came to the gate of the court, I saw better of what sort was the building I had arrived at. There was a square yard with monstrous high walls, at the left of which was the main block of the house, and on the right what I took to be the byres and stables. The place looked ancient, and the stone in many places was crumbling away; but the style was of yesterday and in no way differing from that of a hundred steadings in the land. There were some kind of arms above the gateway, and a bit of an iron stanchion; and when I had my sheep inside of it, I saw that the court was all grown up with green grass. And what seemed queer in that dusky half-light was the want of sound. There was no neichering of horses, nor routing of kye, nor clack of hens, but all as still as the top of Ben Cruachan. It was warm and pleasant, too, though the night was chill without.

'I had no sooner entered the place than a row of sheep-pens caught my eye, fixed against the wall in front. This I thought mighty convenient, so I made all haste to put my beasts into them; and finding that there was a good supply of hay within, I leff them easy in my mind, and turned about to look for the door of the house.

'To my wonder, when I found it, it was open wide to the wall; so, being confident with much whisky, I never took thought to knock, but walked boldly in. There's some careless folk here, thinks I to myself, and I much misdoubt if the man knows aught about farming. He'll maybe just be a town's body taking the air on the muirs.

'The place I entered upon was a hall, not like a muirland farmhouse, but more fine than I had ever seen. It was laid with a verra fine carpet, all red and blue and gay colours, and in the corner in a fireplace a great fire crackled. There were chairs, too, and a walth of old rusty arms on the walls, and all manner of whigmaleeries that folk think ornamental. But nobody was there, so I made for the staircase which was at the further side, and went up it stoutly. I made scarce any noise so thickly was it carpeted, and I will own it kind of terrified me to be walking in such a place. But when a man has drunk well he is troubled not overmuckle with modesty or fear, so I e'en stepped out and soon came to a landing where was a door.

'Now, thinks I, at last I have won to the habitable parts of the house; so laying my finger on the sneck I lifted it and entered. And there before me was the finest room in all the world; indeed I abate not a jot of the phrase, for I cannot think of anything finer. It was hung with braw pictures and lined with big bookcases of oak well-filled with books in fine bindings. The furnishing seemed carved by a skilled hand, and the cushions and curtains were soft velvet. But the best thing was the table, which was covered with a clean white cloth and set with all kind of good meat and drink. The dishes were of silver and as bright as Loch Awe water in an April sun. Eh, but it was a braw braw sight for a drover! And there at the far end, with a great pottle of wine before him, sat the master.

'He rose as I entered, and I saw him to be dressed in the pink of town fashion, a man of maybe fifty years, but hale and well-looking, with a peaked beard and trimmed moustache and thick eyebrows. His eyes were slanted a thought, which is a thing I hate in any man, but his whole appearance was pleasing.

' "Mr Stewart?" says he courteously, looking at me. "Is it Mr Duncan Stewart that I will be indebted to for the honour of this visit?"

'I stared at him blankly, for how did he ken my name?

' "That is my name," I said, "but who the tevil tell't you about it?"

' "Oh, my name is Stewart myself," says he, "and all Stewarts should be well acquaint."

' "True," said I, "though I don't mind your face before. But now I am here, I think you have a most gallant place, Mr Stewart."

' "Well enough. But how have you come to't? We've few visitors."

'So I told him where I had come from, and where I was going, and why I was forwandered at this time of night among the muirs. He listened keenly, and when I had finished, he says verra friendly-like, "Then you'll bide all night and take supper with me. It would never be doing to let one of the clan go away without breaking bread. Sit ye down, Mr Duncan."

'I sat down gladly enough, though I own that at first I did not half-like the whole business. There was something unchristian about the place, and for certain it was not seemly that the man's name should be the same as my own, and that he should be so well posted in my doings. But he seemed so well-disposed that my misgivings soon vanished.

'So I seated myself at the table opposite my entertainer. There was a place laid ready for me, and beside the knife and fork a long horn-handled spoon. I had never seen a spoon so long and queer, and I asked the man what it meant. "Oh," says he, "the broth in this house is very often hot, so we need a long spoon to sup it. It is a common enough thing, is it not?"

'I could answer nothing to this, though it did not seem to me sense, and I had an inkling of something I had heard about long spoons which I thought was not good; but my wits were not clear, as I have told you already. A serving man brought me a great bowl of soup and set it before me. I had hardly plunged spoon intil it, when Mr Stewart cries out from the other end: "Now, Mr Duncan, I call you to witness that you sit down to supper of your own accord. I've an ill name in these parts for compelling folk to take meat with me when they dinna want it. But you'll bear me witness that you're willing."

'"Yes, by God, I am that," I said, for the savoury smell of the broth was rising to my nostrils. The other smiled at this as if well-pleased.

'I have tasted many soups, but I swear there never was one like that. It was as if all the good things in the world

31

were mixed thegether – whisky and kale and shortbread and cocky-leeky and honey and salmon. The taste of it was enough to make a body's heart loup with fair gratitude. The smell of it was like the spicy winds of Arabia, that you read about in the Bible, and when you had taken a spoonful you felt as happy as if you had sellt a hundred yowes at twice their reasonable worth. Oh, it was grand soup!

'"What Stewarts did you say you comed from," I asked my entertainer.

'"Oh," he says, "I'm connected with them all, Athole Stewarts, Appin Stewarts, Rannoch Stewarts; and a' I've a heap o' land thereaways."

'"Whereabouts?" says I, wondering. "Is't at the Blair o' Athole, or along by Tummel side, or wast the Loch o' Rannoch, or on the Muir, or in Mamore?"

'"In all the places you name," says he.

'"Got damn," says I, "then what for do you not bide there instead of in these stinking lawlands?"

'At this he laughed softly to himself. "Why, for maybe the same reason as yoursel, Mr Duncan. You know the proverb, 'A' Stewarts are sib to the Deil.'"

'I laughed loudly; "Oh, you've been a wild one, too, have you? Then you're not worse than mysel. I ken the inside of every public in the Cowgate and Cannongate, and there's not another drover on the road my match at fechting and drinking and dicing." And I started on a long shameless catalogue of my misdeeds. Mr Stewart meantime listened with a satisfied smirk on his face.

' "Yes, I've heard tell of you, Mr Duncan," he says. "But here's something more, and you'll doubtless be hungry."

'And now there was set on the table a round of beef garnished with pot-herbs, all most delicately fine to the taste. From a great cupboard were brought many bottles of wine, and in a massive silver bowl at the table's head were put whisky and lemons and sugar. I do not know well what I drank, but whatever it might be it was the best ever brewed. It made you scarce feel the earth round about you, and you were so happy you could scarce keep from singing. I wad give much siller to this day for the receipt.

'Now, the wine made me talk, and I began to boast of my own great qualities, the things I had done and the things I was going to do. I was a drover just now, but it was not long that I would be being a drover. I had bought a flock of my own, and would sell it for a hundred pounds, no less; with that I would buy a bigger one till I had made money enough to stock a farm; and then I would leave the road and spend my days in peace, seeing to my land and living in good company. Was not my father, I cried, own cousin, thrice removed, to the Macleans o' Duart, and my mother's uncle's wife a Rory of Balnacrory? And I am a scholar too, said I, for I was a matter of two years at Embro' College, and might have been roaring in the pulpit, if I hadna liked the drink and the lassies too well.

' "See," said I, "I will prove it to you;" and I rose from

33

the table and went to one of the bookcases. There were all manner of books, Latin and Greek, poets and philosophers, but in the main, divinity. For there I saw Richard Baxter's "Call to the Unconverted," and Thomas Boston of Ettrick's "Fourfold State," not to speak of the *Sermons* of half a hundred auld ministers, and the "Hind let Loose," and many books of the covenanting folk.

' "Faith," I says, "you've a fine collection, Mr What's-your-name," for the wine had made me free in my talk. "There is many a minister and professor in the Kirk, I'll warrant, who has a less godly library. I begin to suspect you of piety, sir."

' "Does it not behoove us," he answered in an unctuous voice, "to mind the words of Holy Writ that evil communications corrupt good manners, and have an eye to our company? These are all the company I have, except when some stranger such as you honours me with a visit."

'I had meantime been opening a book of plays, I think by the famous William Shakespeare, and I here proke into a loud laugh. "Ha, ha, Mr Stewart," I says, "here's a sentence I've lighted on which is hard on you. Listen! 'The Devil can quote Scripture to advantage.' "

'The other laughed long. "He who wrote that was a shrewd man," he said, "but I'll warrant if you'll open another volume, you'll find some quip on yourself."

'I did as I was bidden, and picked up a white-backed book, and opening it at random, read: "There be many who spend their days in evil and wine-bibbing, in lusting and cheating, who think to mend while yet there is time; but the opportunity is to them for ever awanting, and they go down open-mouthed to the great fire."

'"Psa," I cried, "some wretched preaching book, I will have none of them. Good wine will be better than bad theology." So I sat down once more at the table.

'"You're a clever man, Mr Duncan," he says, "and a well-read one. I commend your spirit in breaking away from the bands of the kirk and the college, though your father was so thrawn against you."

'"Enough of that," I said, "though I don't know who told you;" I was angry to hear my father spoken of, as though the grieving him was a thing to be proud of.

'"Oh, as you please," he says; "I was just going to say that I commended your spirit in sticking the knife into the man in the Pleasaunce, the time you had to hide for a month about the backs o' Leith."

'"How do you ken that," I asked hotly, "you've heard more about me than ought to be repeated, let me tell you."

'"Don't be angry," he said sweetly; "I like you well for these things, and you mind the lassie in Athole that was so fond of you. You treated her well, did you not?"

'I made no answer, being too much surprised at his knowledge of things which I thought none knew but myself.

'"Oh yes, Mr Duncan. I could tell you what you were doing to-day, how you cheated Jock Gallowa out of six pounds, and sold a horse to the farmer of Haypath that was scarce fit to carry him home. And I know what you are meaning to do the morn at Glesca, and I wish you well of it."

' "I think you must be the Devil," I said blankly.

' "The same, at your service," said he, still smiling.

'I looked at him in terror, and even as I looked I kenned by something in his eyes and the twitch of his lips that he was speaking the truth.

' "And what place is this, you . . ." I stammered.

' "Call me Mr S.," he says gently, "and enjoy your stay while you are here and don't concern yourself about the lawing."

' "The lawing!" I cried in astonishment, "and is this a house of public entertainment?"

' "To be sure, else how is a poor man to live?"

' "Name it," said I, "and I will pay and be gone."

' "Well," said he, "I make it a habit to give a man his choice. In your case it will be your wealth or your chances hereafter, in plain English your flock or your —"

' "My immortal soul," I gasped.

' "Your soul," said Mr S., bowing, "though I think you call it by too flattering an adjective."

' "You damned thief," I roared, "you would entice a man into your accursed house and then strip him bare."

' "Hold hard," said he, "don't let us spoil our good fellowship by incivilities. And, mind you, I took you to witness to begin with that you sat down of your own accord."

' "So you did," said I, and could say no more.

' "Come, come," he says, "don't take it so bad. You may keep all your gear and yet part from here in safety. You've but to sign your name, which is no hard task to a college-bred man, and go on living as you live just now to the end. And let me tell you, Mr Duncan Stewart, that you should take it as a great obligement that I am willing to take your bit soul instead of fifty sheep. There's no many would value it so high."

' "Maybe no, maybe no," I said sadly, "but it's all I have. D'ye no see that if I gave it up, there would be no chance left of mending? And I'm sure I do not want your company to all eternity."

' "Faith, that's uncivil," he says; "I was just about to say that we had had a very pleasant evening."

'I sat back in my chair very down-hearted. I must leave this place as poor as a kirk-mouse, and begin again with little but the clothes on my back. I was strongly tempted to sign the bit paper thing and have done with it all, but somehow I could not bring myself to do it. So at last I says to him: "Well, I've made up my mind. I'll give you my sheep, sorry though I be to lose them, and I hope I may never come near this place again as long as I live."

' "On the contrary," he said, "I hope often to have the pleasure of your company. And seeing that you've paid well for your lodging, I hope you'll make the best of it. Don't be sparing on the drink."

'I looked hard at him for a second. "You've an ill name,

37

and an ill trade, but you're no a bad sort yoursel, and, do you ken, I like you."

' "I'm much obliged to you for the character," says he, "and I'll take your hand on't."

'So I filled up my glass and we set to, and such an evening I never mind of. We never got fou, but just in a fine good temper and very entertaining. The stories we told and the jokes we cracked are still a kind of memory with me, though I could not come over one of them. And then, when I got sleepy, I was shown to the brawest bedroom, all hung with pictures and looking-glasses, and with bed-clothes of the finest linen and a coverlet of silk. I bade Mr S. good-night, and my head was scarce on the pillow ere I was sound asleep.

'When I awoke the sun was just newly risen, and the frost of a September morning was on my clothes. I was lying among green braes with nothing near me but crying whaups and heathery hills, and my two dogs running round about and howling as they were mad.'

The Comedy-Ballet of Marionnettes, as performed by the troupe of the Théâtre Impossible

In a Gallery

PORTRAIT OF A LADY (UNKNOWN)

By Katharine de Mattos

Veiled eyes, yet quick to meet one glance
    Not his, not yours, but *mine*,
Lips that are fain to stir and breathe
    Dead joys (not love nor wine):
'Tis not in *you* the secret lurks
    That makes men pause and pass!

Did unseen magic flow from you
Long since to madden hearts,
And those who loathed remain to pray
And work their dolorous parts –
To seek your riddle, dread or sweet,
    And find it in the grave?

Till some one painted you one day,
Perchance to ease his soul,
And set you here to weave your spells
While time and silence roll;
And you were hungry for the hour
    When one should understand?

In a Gallery

Your jewelled fingers writhe and gleam
From out your sombre vest;
Am I the first of those who gaze,
Who may their meaning guess,
Yet dare not whisper lest the words
Pale even painted cheeks?

Portrait of Mrs Patrick Campbell

The Pleasure-Pilgrim

By Ella D'Arcy

I

Campbell was on his way to Schloss Altenau, for a second quiet season with his work. He had spent three profitable months there a year ago, and now he was devoutly hoping for a repetition of that good fortune. His thoughts outran the train; and long before his arrival at the Hamelin railway station, he was enjoying his welcome by the Ritterhausens, was revelling in the ease and comfort of the old castle, and was contrasting the pleasures of his home-coming – for he looked upon Schloss Altenau as a sort of temporary home – with his recent cheerless experiences of lodging-houses in London, hotels in Berlin, and strange indifferent faces everywhere. He thought with especial satisfaction of the Maynes, and of the good talks Mayne and he would have together, late at night, before the great fire in the hall, after the rest of the household had gone to bed. He blessed the adverse circumstances which had turned Schloss Altenau into a boarding-house, and had reduced the Freiherr Ritterhausen to eke out his shrunken revenues by the reception, as paying guests, of English and American pleasure-pilgrims.

He rubbed the blurred window-pane with the fringed end of the strap hanging from it, and, in the snow-covered landscape reeling towards him, began to recognise objects that were familiar. Hamelin could not be far off . . . In another ten minutes the train came to a standstill.

He stepped down from the overheated atmosphere of his compartment into the cold bright February afternoon, and through the open station doors saw one of the Ritterhausen carriages awaiting him, with Gottlieb in his second-best livery on the box. Gottlieb showed every reasonable consideration for the Baron's boarders, but he had various methods of marking his sense of the immense abyss separating them from the family. The use of his second-best livery was one of these methods. Nevertheless, he turned a friendly German eye up to Campbell, and in response to his cordial 'Guten Tag, Gottlieb. Wie geht's? Und die Herrschaften?' expressed his pleasure at seeing the young man back again.

While Campbell stood at the top of the steps that led down to the carriage and the Platz, looking after the collection of his luggage and its bestowal by Gottlieb's side, he became aware of two persons, ladies, advancing towards him from the direction of the Wartsaal. It was surprising to see any one at any time in Hamelin station. It was still more surprising when one of these ladies addressed him by name.

'You are Mr Campbell, are you not?' she said. 'We have been waiting for you to go back in the carriage together. When we found this morning that there was only half-an-hour between your train and ours, I told the Baroness it would be perfectly absurd to send to the station twice. I hope you won't mind our company?'

The first impression Campbell received was of the magnificent apparel of the lady before him; it would have been noticeable in Paris or Vienna – it was extravagant here. Next, he perceived that the face beneath the upstanding feathers and the curving hat-brim was that of so very young a girl as to make the furs and velvets seem more incongruous still. But the incongruity vanished with the intonation of her first phrase, which told him she was an American. He had no standards for American dress or manners. It was clear that the speaker and her companion were inmates of the Schloss.

Campbell bowed, and murmured the pleasure he did not feel. A true Briton, he was intolerably shy; and his heart sank at the prospect of a three-mile drive with two strangers who evidently had the advantage of knowing all about him, while he was in ignorance of their very names. As he took his place opposite to them in the carriage, he unconsciously assumed a cold blank stare, pulling nervously at his moustache, as was his habit in moments of discomposure. Had his companions been British also, the ordeal of the drive would certainly have been a terrible one; but these young American girls showed no sense of embarrassment whatever.

'We've just come back from Hanover,' said the one who had already spoken to him. 'I go over once a week for a singing lesson, and my little sister comes along to take care of me.'

She turned a narrow, smiling glance from Campbell to her little sister, and then back to Campbell again. She had red hair, freckles on her nose, and the most singular eyes he had ever seen; slit-like eyes, set obliquely in her head, Chinese fashion.

'Yes, Lulie requires a great deal of taking care of,' assented the little sister, sedately, though the way in which she said it seemed to imply something less simple than the words themselves. The speaker bore no resemblance to Lulie. She was smaller, thinner, paler. Her features were straight, a trifle peaked; her skin sallow; her hair of a nondescript brown. She was much less gorgeously dressed. There was even a suggestion of shabbiness in her attire, though sundry isolated details of it were handsome too. She was also much less young; or so, at any rate, Campbell began by pronouncing her. Yet presently he wavered. She had a face that defied you to fix her age. Campbell never fixed it to his own satisfaction, but veered in the course of that drive (as he was destined to do during the next few weeks) from point to point up and down the scale between eighteen and thirty-five. She wore a spotted veil, and beneath it a pince-nez, the lenses of which did something to temper the immense amount of humorous meaning which lurked in her gaze. When her pale prominent eyes met Campbell's, it seemed to the young man that they were full of eagerness to add something at his expense to the stores of information they had already garnered up. They chilled him with misgivings; there was more comfort to be found in her sister's shifting red-brown glances.

'Hanover is a long way to go for lessons,' he observed, forcing himself to be conversational. 'I used to go myself about once a week, when I first came to Schloss Altenau, for tobacco, or notepaper, or to get my hair cut. But later on I did without, or contented myself with what Hamelin, or even the village, could offer me.'

'Nannie and I,' said the young girl, 'meant to stay only a week at Altenau, on our way to Hanover, where we were going to pass the winter; but the Castle is just too lovely for anything,' she added softly. She raised her eyelids the least little bit as she looked at him, and such a warm and friendly gaze shot out that Campbell was suddenly thrilled. Was she pretty, after all? He glanced at Nannie; she, at least, was indubitably plain. 'It's the very first time we've ever stayed in a castle,' Lulie went on; 'and we're going to remain right along now, until we go home in the spring. Just imagine living in a house with a real moat, and a drawbridge, and a Rittersaal, and suits of

49

armour that have been actually worn in battle! And oh, that delightful iron collar and chain! You remember it, Mr Campbell? It hangs right close to the gateway on the court-yard side. And you know, in old days, the Ritterhausens used it for the punishment of their serfs. There are horrible stories connected with it. Mr Mayne can tell you them. But just think of being chained up there like a dog! So wonderfully picturesque.'

'For the spectator perhaps,' said Campbell, smiling. 'I doubt if the victim appreciated the picturesque aspect of the case.'

With this Lulie disagreed. 'Oh, I think he must have been interested,' she said. 'It must have made him feel so absolutely part and parcel of the Middle Ages. I persuaded Mr Mayne to fix the collar round my neck the other day; and though it was very uncomfortable, and I had to stand on tiptoe, it seemed to me that all at once the court-yard was filled with knights in armour, and crusaders, and palmers, and things; and there were flags flying and trumpets sounding; and all the dead and gone Ritterhausens had come down from their picture-frames, and were walking about in brocaded gowns and lace ruffles.'

'It seemed to require a good deal of persuasion to get Mr Mayne to unfix the collar again,' said the little sister. 'How at last did you manage it?'

But Lulie replied irrelevantly: 'And the Ritterhausens are such perfectly lovely people, aren't they, Mr Campbell?

The old Baron is a perfect dear. He has such a grand manner. When he kisses my hand I feel nothing less than a princess. And the Baroness is such a funny, busy, delicious little round ball of a thing. And she's always playing bagatelle, isn't she? Or else cutting up skeins of wool for carpet-making.' She meditated a moment. 'Some people always *are* cutting things up in order to join them together again,' she announced, in her fresh drawling little voice.

'And some people cut things up, and leave other people to do all the reparation,' commented the little sister, enigmatically.

And all this time the carriage had been rattling over the cobble-paved streets of the quaint mediæval town, where the houses stand so near together that you may shake hands with your opposite neighbour; where allegorical figures, strange birds and beasts, are carved and painted over the windows and doors; and where to every distant sound you lean your ear to catch the fairy music of the Pied Piper, and at every street corner you look to see his tatterdemalion form with the frolicking children at his heels.

Then the Weser bridge was crossed, beneath which the ice-floes jostled and ground themselves together, as they forced a way down the river; and the carriage was rolling smoothly along country roads, between vacant snow-decked fields.

Campbell's embarrassment was wearing off. Now that

he was getting accustomed to the girls, he found neither
of them awe-inspiring. The red-haired one had a simple
child-like manner that was charming. Her strange little
face, with its piquant irregularity of line, its warmth of
colour, began to please him. What though her hair was
red, the uncurled wisp which strayed across her white
forehead was soft and alluring; he could see soft masses
of it tucked up beneath her hat-brim as she turned her
head. When she suddenly lifted her red-brown lashes,
those queer eyes of hers had a velvety softness too.
Decidedly, she struck him as being pretty – in a peculiar
way. He felt an immense accession of interest in her. It
seemed to him that he was the discoverer of her possibil-
ities. He did not doubt that the rest of the world called
her plain, or at least odd-looking. He, at first, had only
seen the freckles on her nose, her oblique-set eyes. He
wondered what she thought of herself, and how she
appeared to Nannie. Probably as a very commonplace
little girl; sisters stand too close to see each other's qualities. She was too young to have had much opportunity
of hearing flattering truths from strangers; and, besides,
the ordinary stranger would see nothing in her to call
for flattering truths. Her charm was something subtle,
out-of-the-common, in defiance of all known rules of
beauty. Campbell saw superiority in himself for recognis-
ing it, for formulating it; and he was not displeased to be
aware that it would always remain caviare to the
multitude.

II

'I'm jolly glad to have you back,' Mayne said, that same evening, when, the rest of the boarders having retired to their rooms, he and Campbell were lingering over the hall-fire for a talk and smoke. 'I've missed you awfully, old chap, and the good times we used to have here. I've often meant to write to you, but you know how one shoves off letter-writing day after day, till at last one is too ashamed of one's indolence to write at all. But tell me – you had a pleasant drive from Hamelin? What do you think of our young ladies?'

'Those American girls? But they're charming,' said Campbell, with enthusiasm. 'The red-haired one is particularly charming.'

At this Mayne laughed so oddly that Campbell questioned him in surprise. 'Isn't she charming?'

'My dear chap,' said Mayne, 'the red-haired one, as you call her, is the most remarkably charming young person I've ever met or read of. We've had a good many American girls here before now – you remember the good old Clamp family, of course? – they were here in your time, I think? – but we've never had anything like this Miss Lulie Thayer. She is something altogether unique.'

Campbell was struck with the name. 'Lulie – Lulie Thayer,' he repeated. 'How pretty it is.' And, full of his great discovery, he felt he must confide it to Mayne,

53

at least. 'Do you know,' he went on, '*she* is really very pretty too? I didn't think so at first, but after a bit I discovered that she is positively quite pretty – in an odd sort of way.'

Mayne laughed again. 'Pretty, pretty!' he echoed in derision. 'Why, *lieber Gott im Himmel*, where are your eyes? Pretty! The girl is beautiful, gorgeously beautiful; every trait, every tint, is in complete, in absolute harmony with the whole. But the truth is, of course, we've all grown accustomed to the obvious, the commonplace; to violent contrasts; blue eyes, black eyebrows, yellow hair; the things that shout for recognition. You speak of Miss Thayer's hair as red. What other colour would you have, with that warm creamy skin? And then, what a red it is! It looks as though it had been steeped in red wine.'

'Ah, what a good description,' said Campbell, appreciatively. 'That's just it – steeped in red wine.'

'And yet it's not so much her beauty,' Mayne continued. 'After all, one has met beautiful women before now. It's her wonderful generosity, her complaisance. She doesn't keep her good things to herself. She doesn't condemn you to admire from a distance.'

'How do you mean?' Campbell asked, surprised again.

'Why, she's the most egregious little flirt I've ever met. And yet, she's not exactly a flirt, either. I mean she doesn't flirt in the ordinary way. She doesn't talk much, or laugh, or apparently make the least claims on masculine attention. And so all the women like her. I don't believe there's one, except my wife, who has an inkling as to her true character. The Baroness, as you know, never observes anything. *Seigneur Dieu!* if she knew the things I could tell her about Miss Lulie! For I've had opportunities of studying her. You see, I'm a married man, and not in my first youth; out of the running altogether. The looker-on gets the best view of the game. But you, who are young and charming and already famous – we've had your book here, by the bye, and there's good stuff in it – you're going to have no end of pleasant experiences. I can see she means to add you to her ninety-and-nine other spoils; I saw it from the way she looked at you at dinner. She always begins with those velvety red-brown glances. She began that way with March and Prendergast and Willie Anson, and all the men we've had here since her arrival. The next thing she'll do will be to press your hand under the tablecloth.'

'Oh, come, Mayne; you're joking,' cried Campbell, a little brusquely. He thought such jokes in bad taste. He had a high ideal of Woman, an immense respect for her; he could not endure to hear her belittled even in jest. 'Miss Thayer is refined and charming. No girl of her class would do such things.'

'What is her class? Who knows anything about her? All we know is that she and her uncanny little friend – her little sister, as she calls her, though they're no more sisters than you and I are – they're not even related – all we know is that she and Miss Dodge (that's the little sister's name) arrived here one memorable day last October from the Kronprinz Hotel at Waldeck-Pyrmont. By the bye, it was the Clamps, I believe, who told her of the Castle – hotel acquaintances – you know how travelling Americans always cotton to each other. And we've picked up a few little biographical notes from her and Miss Dodge since. *Zum Beispiel*, she's got a rich father somewhere away back in Michigan, who supplies her with all the money she wants. And she's been travelling about since last May: Paris, Vienna, the Rhine, Düsseldorf, and so on here. She must have had some rich experiences, by Jove. For she's done everything. Cycled in Paris: you should see her in her cycling costume; she wears it when the Baron takes her out shooting – she's an admirable shot, by the way, an accomplishment learned, I suppose, from some American cow-boy. Then in Berlin she did a month's hospital nursing; and now she's studying the higher branches of the Terpsichorean art. You know she was in Hanover to-day. Did she tell you what she went for?'

'To take a singing lesson,' said Campbell, remembering the reason she had given.

'A singing lesson! Do you sing with your legs? A dancing lesson, *mein lieber*. A dancing lesson from the ballet-master of the Hof Theater. She could deposit a kiss on your forehead with her foot, I don't doubt. I wonder if she can do the *grand écart* yet.' And when Campbell, in astonishment, wondered why on earth she should wish to do such things, 'Oh, to extend her opportunities,' Mayne explained, 'and to acquire fresh sensations. She's an adventuress. Yes, an adventuress, but an end-of-the-century one. She doesn't travel for profit, but for pleasure. She has no desire to swindle her neighbour of dollars, but to amuse herself at his expense. And she's clever; she's read a good deal; she knows how to apply her reading to practical life. Thus, she's learned from Herrick not to be coy; and from Shakespeare that sweet-and-twenty is the time for kissing and being kissed. She honours her masters in the observance. She was not in the least abashed when, one day, I suddenly came upon her teaching that damned idiot, young Anson, two new ways of kissing.'

Campbell's impressions of the girl were readjusting themselves completely, but for the moment he was unconscious of the change. He only knew that he was partly angry, partly incredulous, and inclined to believe that Mayne was chaffing him.

'But Miss Dodge,' he objected, 'the little sister, she is older; old enough to look after her friend. Surely she could not allow a young girl placed in her charge to behave in such a way—'

'Oh, that little Dodge girl,' said Mayne contemptuously; 'Miss Thayer pays the whole shot, I understand, and Miss Dodge plays gooseberry, sheep-dog, jackal, what you will. She finds her reward in the other's cast-off finery. The silk blouse she was wearing to-night, I've good

57

reason for remembering, belonged to Miss Lulie. For, during a brief season, I must tell you, my young lady had the caprice to show attentions to your humble servant. I suppose my being a married man lent me a factitious fascination. But I didn't see it. That kind of girl doesn't appeal to me. So she employed Miss Dodge to do a little active canvassing. It was really too funny; I was coming in one day after a walk in the woods; my wife was trimming bonnets, or had neuralgia, or something. Anyhow, I was alone, and Miss Dodge contrived to waylay me in the middle of the court-yard. "Don't you find it vurry dull walking all by yourself?" she asked me; and then blinking up in her strange little short-sighted way – she's really the weirdest little creature – "Why don't you make love to Lulie?" she said; "you'd find her vurry charming." It took me a minute or two to recover presence of mind enough to ask her whether Miss Thayer had commissioned her to tell me so. She looked at me with that cryptic smile of hers; "She'd like you to do so, I'm sure," she finally remarked, and pirouetted away. Though it didn't come off, owing to my bashfulness, it was then that Miss Dodge appropriated the silk bodice; and Providence, taking pity on Miss Thayer's forced inactivity, sent along March, a young fellow reading for the army, with whom she had great doings. She fooled him to the top of his bent; sat on his knee; gave him a lock of her hair, which, having no scissors handy, she burned off with a cigarette taken from his mouth; and got him to offer her marriage. Then she turned round and laughed in his face, and took up with a Dr Weber, a cousin of the Baron's, under the other man's very eyes. You never saw anything like the unblushing coolness with which she would permit March to catch her in Weber's arms.'

'Come,' Campbell protested, 'aren't you drawing it rather strong?'

'On the contrary, I'm drawing it mild, as you'll discover presently for yourself; and then you'll thank me for fore-warning you. For she makes love – desperate love, mind you – to every man she meets. And goodness knows how many she hasn't met, in the course of her career, which began presumably at the age of ten, in some "Amur'can" hotel or watering-place. Look at this.' Mayne fetched an alpenstock from a corner of the hall; it was decorated with a long succession of names, which, ribbon-like, were twisted round and round it, carved in the wood. 'Read them,' insisted Mayne, putting the stick in Campbell's hands. 'You'll see they're not the names of the peaks she has climbed, or the towns she has passed through; they're the names of the men she has fooled. And there's room for more; there's still a good deal of space, as you see. There's room for yours.'

Campbell glanced down the alpenstock – reading here a name, there an initial, or just a date – and jerked it impatiently from him on to a couch. He wished with all his heart that Mayne would stop, would talk of something else, would let him get away. The young girl had interested him so much; he had felt himself so drawn towards her; he had thought her so fresh, so innocent. But Mayne, on the contrary, was warming to his subject, was enchanted to have some one to listen to his stories, to discuss his theories, to share his cynical amusement.

'I don't think, mind you,' he said, 'that she is a bit interested herself in the men she flirts with. I don't think she gets any of the usual sensations from it, you know. I think she just does it for devilry, for a laugh. Sometimes I wonder whether she does it with an idea of retribution. Perhaps some woman she was fond of, perhaps her mother even – who knows? – was badly treated at the hands of a man. Perhaps this girl has constituted herself the Nemesis for her sex, and goes about seeing how many masculine hearts she can break by way of revenge. Or can it be that she is simply the newest development of the New Woman – she who in England preaches and bores you, and in America practises and pleases? Yes, I believe she's the American edition, and so new that she hasn't yet found her way into fiction. She's the pioneer of the army coming out of the West, that's going to destroy the existing scheme of things and rebuild it nearer to the heart's desire.'

'Oh, damn it all, Mayne,' cried Campbell, rising abruptly, 'why not say at once that she's a wanton, and have done with it? Who wants to hear your rotten theories?' And he lighted his candle without another word, and went off to bed.

III

It was four o'clock, and the Baron's boarders were drinking their afternoon coffee, drawn up in a circle round the hall-fire. All but Campbell, who had carried his cup away to a side-table, and, with a book open before him, appeared to be reading assiduously. In reality he could not follow a line of what he read; he could not keep his thoughts from Miss Thayer. What Mayne had told him was germinating in his mind. Knowing his friend as he did, he could not on reflection doubt his word. In spite of much superficial cynicism, Mayne was incapable of speaking lightly of any young girl without good cause. It now seemed to Campbell that, instead of exaggerating the case, Mayne had probably understated it. The girl repelled him to-day as much as she had charmed him yesterday. He asked himself with horror, what had she not already known, seen, permitted? When now and again his eyes travelled over, perforce, to where she sat, her red head leaning against Miss Dodge's knee, seeming to attract and concentrate all the glow of the fire, his forehead set itself in frowns, and he returned with an increased sense of irritation to his book.

'I'm just sizzling up, Nannie,' Miss Thayer presently complained, in her child-like, drawling little way; 'this fire is too hot for anything.' She rose and shook straight her loose tea-gown, a marvellous garment created in

Paris, which would have accused a duchess of wilful extravagance. She stood smiling round a moment, pulling on and off with her right hand the big diamond ring which decorated the left. At the sound of her voice Campbell had looked up; now his cold unfriendly eyes encountered hers. He glanced rapidly past her, then back to his book. But she, undeterred, with a charming sinuous movement and a frou-frou of trailing silks, crossed over towards him. She slipped into an empty chair next his.

'I'm going to do you the honour of sitting beside you, Mr Campbell,' she said sweetly.

'It's an honour I've done nothing whatever to merit,' he answered, without looking at her, and turned a page.

'The right retort,' she approved; 'but you might have said it a little more cordially.'

'I don't feel cordial.'

'But why not? What has happened? Yesterday you were so nice.'

'Ah, a good deal of water has run under the bridge since yesterday.'

'But still the river remains as full,' she told him, smiling, 'and still the sky is as blue. The thermometer has even risen six degrees. Out-of-doors, to-day, I could feel the spring-time in the air. You, too, love the spring, don't you? I know that from your books. And I wanted to tell you, I think your books perfectly lovely. I know them, most all. I've read them away home. They're very much thought of in America. Only last night I was saying to Nannie how glad I am to have met you, for I think we're going to be great friends; aren't we, Mr Campbell? At least, I hope so, for you can do me so much good, if you will. Your books always make me feel real good; but you yourself can help me much more.'

She looked up at him with one of her warm, narrow red-brown glances, which yesterday would have thrilled his blood, and to-day merely stirred it to anger.

'You over-estimate my abilities,' he said coldly; 'and on the whole, I fear you will find writers a very disappointing race. You see, they put their best into their books. So, not to disillusion you too rapidly' – he rose – 'will you excuse me? I have some work to do.' And he left her sitting there alone.

But he did no work when he got to his room. Whether Lulie Thayer was actually present or not, it seemed that her influence was equally disturbing to him. His mind was full of her: of her singular eyes, her quaint intonation, her sweet seductive praise. Yesterday such praise would have been delightful to him: what young author is proof against appreciation of his books? To-day, Campbell simply told himself that she laid the butter on too thick; that it was in some analogous manner she had flattered up March, Anson, and all the rest of the men that Mayne had spoken of. He supposed it was the first step in the process by which he was to be fooled, twisted round her finger, added to the list of victims who strewed her conquering path. He had a special fear of being fooled. For beneath a somewhat supercilious exterior, the dominant note of his character was timidity, distrust of his own merits; and he knew he was single-minded – one-idea'd almost; if he were to let himself go, to get to care very much for a woman, for such a girl as this girl, for instance, he would lose himself completely, be at her mercy absolutely. Fortunately, Mayne had let him know her character: he could feel nothing but dislike for her – disgust, even; and yet he was conscious how pleasant it would be to believe in her innocence, in her candour. For she was so adorably pretty: her flower-like beauty grew upon him; her head, drooping a little on one side when she looked up, was so like a flower bent by its own weight. The texture of her cheeks, her lips, were delicious as the petals of a flower. He found he could recall with perfect accuracy every detail of her appearance: the manner in which the red hair grew round her temples; how it was loosely and gracefully fastened up behind with just a single tortoise-shell pin. He recalled the suspicion of a dimple which shadowed itself in her cheek when she spoke, and deepened into a delicious reality every time she smiled. He remembered her throat; her hands, of a beautiful whiteness, with pink palms and pointed fingers. It was impossible to write. He speculated long on the ring she wore on her engaged finger. He mentioned this ring to Mayne the next time he saw him.

'Engaged? very much so I should say. Has got a *fiancé*

in every capital of Europe probably. But the ring-man is the *fiancé en titre*. He writes to her by every mail, and is tremendously in love with her. She shows me his letters. When she's had her fling, I suppose, she'll go back and marry him. That's what these little American girls do, I'm told; sow their wild oats here with us, and settle down into *bonnes ménagères* over yonder. Meanwhile, are you having any fun with her? Aha, she presses your hand? The "gesegnete Mahlzeit" business after dinner is an excellent institution, isn't it? She'll tell you how much she loves you soon; that's the next move in the game.'

But so far she had done none of these things, for Campbell gave her no opportunities. He was guarded in the extreme, ungenial; avoiding her even at the cost of civility. Sometimes he was downright rude. That especially occurred when he felt himself inclined to yield to her advances. For she made him all sorts of silent advances, speaking with her eyes, her sad little mouth, her beseeching attitude. And then one evening she went further still. It occurred after dinner in the little green drawing-room. The rest of the company were gathered together in the big drawing-room beyond. The small room has deep embrasures to the windows. Each embrasure holds two old faded green velvet sofas in black oaken frames, and an oaken oblong table stands between them. Campbell had flung himself down on one of these sofas in the corner nearest the window. Miss Thayer, passing through the room, saw him, and sat down opposite. She leaned her elbows on the table, the laces of her sleeves falling away from her round white arms, and clasped her hands.

'Mr Campbell, tell me what have I done? How have I vexed you? You have hardly spoken two words to me all day. You always try to avoid me.' And when he began to utter evasive banalities, she stopped him with an imploring 'Don't! I love you. You know I love you. I love you so much I can't bear you to put me off with mere phrases.'

Campbell admired the well-simulated passion in her voice, remembered Mayne's prediction, and laughed aloud.

'Oh, you may laugh,' she said, 'but I am serious. I love you, I love you with my whole soul.' She slipped round the end of the table, and came close beside him. His first impulse was to rise; then he resigned himself to stay. But it was not so much resignation that was required, as self-mastery, cool-headedness. Her close proximity, her fragrance, those wonderful eyes raised so beseechingly to his, made his heart beat.

'Why are you so cold?' she said. 'I love you so; can't you love me a little too?'

'My dear young lady,' said Campbell, gently repelling her, 'what do you take me for? A foolish boy like your friends Anson and March? What you are saying is monstrous, preposterous. Ten days ago you'd never even seen me.'

'What has length of time to do with it?' she said. 'I loved you at first sight.'

'I wonder,' he observed judicially, and again gently removed her hand from his, 'to how many men you have not already said the same thing.'

'I've never meant it before,' she said quite earnestly, and nestled closer to him, and kissed the breast of his coat, and held her mouth up towards his. But he kept his chin resolutely high, and looked over her head.

'How many men have you not already kissed, even since you've been here?'

'But there've not been many here to kiss!' she exclaimed naïvely.

'Well, there was March; you kissed him?'

'No, I'm quite sure I didn't.'

'And young Anson; what about him? Ah, you don't answer! And then the other fellow – what's his name – Prendergast – you've kissed him?'

'But, after all, what is there in a kiss?' she cried ingenuously. 'It means nothing, absolutely nothing. Why, one has to kiss all sorts of people one doesn't care about.'

Campbell remembered how Mayne had said she had probably known strange kisses since the age of ten; and a wave of anger with her, of righteous indignation, rose within him.

'To me,' said he, 'to all right-thinking people, a young girl's kisses are something pure, something sacred, not to be offered indiscriminately to every fellow she meets.

Ah, you don't know what you have lost! You have seen a fruit that has been handled, that has lost its bloom? You have seen primroses, spring flowers gathered and thrown away in the dust? And who enjoys the one, or picks up the others? And this is what you remind me of – only you have deliberately, of your own perverse will, tarnished your beauty, and thrown away all the modesty, the reticence, the delicacy, which make a young girl so infinitely dear. You revolt me, you disgust me. I want nothing from you, but to be let alone. Kindly take your hands away, and let me go.'

He roughly shook her off and got up, then felt a moment's curiosity to see how she would take the repulse.

Miss Thayer never blushed: had never, he imagined, in her life done so. No faintest trace of colour now stained the warm pallor of her rose-leaf skin; but her eyes filled up with tears; two drops gathered on the under-lashes, grew large, trembled an instant, and then rolled unchecked down her cheeks. Those tears somehow put him in the wrong, and he felt he had behaved brutally to her for the rest of the night.

He began to find excuses for her: after all, she meant no harm: it was her up-bringing, her *genre*: it was a *genre* he loathed; but perhaps he need not have spoken so harshly to her. He thought he would find a more friendly word for her next morning; and he loitered about the Mahlsaal, where the boarders come in to breakfast as in an hotel, just when it suits them, till past eleven; but the girl never turned up. Then, when he was almost tired of waiting, Miss Dodge put in an appearance, in a flannel wrapper, and her front hair twisted up in steel pins.

Campbell judged Miss Dodge with even more severity than he did Miss Thayer; there was nothing in this weird little creature's appearance to temper justice with mercy. It was with difficulty that he brought himself to inquire after her friend.

'Lulie is sick this morning,' she told him. 'I've come down to order her some broth. She couldn't sleep any last night, because of your unkindness to her. She's vurry, vurry unhappy about it.'

'Yes, I'm sorry for what I said. I had no right to speak so strongly, I suppose. But I spoke strongly because I feel strongly. However, there's no reason why my bad manners should make her unhappy.'

'Oh, yes, there's vurry good reason,' said Miss Dodge. 'She's vurry much in love with you.'

Campbell looked at the speaker long and earnestly to try and read her mind; but the prominent blinking eyes, the cryptic physiognomy, told him nothing.

'Look here,' he said brusquely, 'what's your object in trying to fool me like this? I know all about your friend. Mayne has told me. She has cried "Wolf" too often before to expect to be believed now.'

'But after all,' argued Miss Dodge, blinking more than ever behind her glasses, 'the wolf did really come at last, you know; didn't he? Lulie is really in love this time.

We've all made mistakes in our lives, haven't we? But that's no reason for not being right at last. And Lulie has cried herself sick.'

Campbell was a little shaken. He went and repeated the conversation to Mayne, who laughed derisively.

'Capital, capital!' he cried; 'excellently contrived. It quite supports my latest theory about our young friend. She's an actress, a born comédienne. She acts always, and to every one: to you, to me, to the Ritterhausens, to the Dodge girl – even to herself when she is quite alone. And she has a great respect for her art; she'll carry out her rôle, *côute que côute*, to the bitter end. She chooses to pose as in love with you; you don't respond; the part now requires that she should sicken and pine. Consequently she takes to her bed, and sends her confidante to tell you so. Oh, it's colossal, it's *famos*.'

IV

'If you can't really love me,' said Lulie Thayer – 'and I know I've been a bad girl and don't deserve that you should – at least, will you allow me to go on loving you?'

She walked by Campbell's side, through the solitary uncared-for park of Schloss Altenau. It was three weeks later in the year, and the spring feeling in the air stirred the blood. All round were signs and tokens of spring: in the busy gaiety of bird and insect life; in the purple flower-tufts which thickened the boughs of the ash trees; in the young green things pushing up pointed heads from amidst last season's dead leaves and grasses. The snow-wreathes, that had for so long decorated the distant hills, were shrinking perceptibly away beneath the strong March sunshine.

There was every invitation to spend one's time out of doors, and Campbell passed long mornings in the park, or wandering through the woods or the surrounding villages. Miss Thayer often accompanied him. He never invited her to do so, but when she offered him her company, he could not, or at least did not, refuse it.

'May I love you? Say,' she entreated.

'"Wenn ich Dich liebe, was geht's Dich an?"' he quoted lightly. 'Oh, no, it's nothing to me, of course. Only don't expect me to believe you – that's all.'

This disbelief of his was the recurring decimal of their conversation. No matter on what subject they began, they always ended thus. And the more sceptical he showed himself, the more eager she became. She exhausted herself in endeavours to convince him.

They had reached the corner in the park where the road to the castle turns off at right angles from the road to Dürrendorf. The ground rises gently on the park-side to within three feet of the top of the wall, although on the other side there is a drop of at least twenty feet. The broad wall-top makes a convenient seat. Campbell and the girl sat down on it. At his last words she wrung her hands together in her lap.

'But how can you disbelieve me?' she cried, 'when I tell you I love you, I adore you? When I swear it to you? And can't you see for yourself? Why, every one at the Castle sees it.'

'Yes, you afford the Castle a good deal of unnecessary amusement. And that shows you don't understand what love really is. Real love is full of delicacy, of reticences, and would feel itself profaned if it became the jest of the servants' hall.'

'I think it's not so much my love for you,' said Lulie gently, 'as your rejection of it, which has made me talked about.'

'No; isn't it rather on account of the favours you've lavished on all my predecessors?'

She sprang from the wall to her feet, and walked up and down in agitation.

'But after all, surely, mistakes of that sort are not to be counted against us? I did really think I was in love with Mr March. Willie Anson doesn't count. He's an American too, and he understands things. Besides, he is only a boy. And how could I know I should love you before I had met you? And how can I help loving you now I have? You're so different from other men. You're good. You're honourable, you treat women with respect. Oh, I do love you so, I do love you! Ask Nannie if I don't.'

The way in which Campbell shrugged his shoulders

clearly expressed the amount of reliance he would place on any testimony from Miss Dodge. He could not forget her 'Why don't you make love to Lulie?' addressed to a married man. Such a want of principle argued an equal want of truth.

Lulie seemed on the brink of weeping.

'Oh, I wish I were dead,' she struggled to say; 'life's impossible if you won't believe me. I don't ask you to love me any longer. I know I've been a bad girl, and I don't deserve that you should; but if you won't believe that I love you, I don't want to live any longer.'

Campbell confessed to himself that she acted admirably, but that the damnable iteration of the one idea became monotonous. He sought a change of subject. 'Look there,' he said, 'close by the wall, what's that jolly little blue flower? It's the first I've seen this year.'

He pointed to where a periwinkle grew at the base of the wall, lifting its bright petals gaily from out its dark glossy leaves.

Lulie, all smiles again, picked it with child-like pleasure. 'Oh, if that's the first you've seen,' she cried, 'you can take a wish. Only you mustn't speak until some one asks you a question.'

She began to fasten it in his coat. 'It's just as blue as your eyes,' she said. 'You have such blue and boyish eyes, you know. Stop, stop, that's not a question,' and seeing that he was about to speak, she laid her finger across his mouth. 'You'll spoil the charm.'

She stepped back, folded her arms, and seemed to dedicate herself to eternal silence; then relenting suddenly:

'Do you believe me?' she entreated.

'What's become of your ring?' Campbell answered irrelevantly. He had noticed its absence from her finger while she had been fixing in the flower.

'Oh, my engagement's broken.'

Campbell asked how the fiancé would like that.

'Oh, he won't mind. He knows I only got engaged because he worried so. And it was always understood between us, that I was to be free if I ever met any one I liked better.'

Campbell asked her what sort of fellow this accommodating fiancé was.

'Oh, he's all right. And he's very good too. But he's not a bit clever, and don't let us talk about him. He makes me tired.'

'But you're wrong,' Campbell told her, 'to throw away a good, a sincere affection. If you really want to reform and turn over a new leaf, as you are always telling me, I should advise you to go home and marry him.'

'What, when I'm in love with you!' she cried reproachfully. 'Would that be right?'

'It's going to rain,' said Campbell. 'Didn't you feel a drop just then? And it's getting near lunch-time. Shall we go in?'

Their shortest way led through the little cemetery in

which the dead and gone Ritterhausens lay at peace, in the shadow of their sometime home.

'When I die the Baron has promised I shall be buried here,' said Lulie pensively; 'just here, next to his first wife. Don't you think it would be lovely to be buried in a beautiful, peaceful baronial graveyard instead of in some horrid crowded city cemetery?'

Mayne met them as they entered the hall. He noticed the flower in his friend's coat. 'Ah, my dear chap, been treading the periwinkle path of dalliance, I see? How many desirable young men have I not witnessed, led down the same broad way by the same seductive lady! Always the same thing, nothing changed, but the flower, according to the season.'

When Campbell reached his room and changed his coat, he threw the flower away into his stove.

Had it not been for Mayne, Miss Thayer might have triumphed after all; might have convinced Campbell of her passion, or have added another victim to her long list. But Mayne had set himself as determinedly to spoil her game as she was bent on winning it. He had always the cynical word, the apt reminiscence ready, whenever he saw signs on Campbell's part of yielding. He was very fond of Campbell. He did not wish to see him fall a prey to the wiles of this little American syren. He had watched her conduct in the past with a dozen different men; he genuinely believed she was only acting now.

Campbell, for his part, began to feel a curious and

growing irritation in the girl's presence. Yet he did not avoid it; he could not well avoid it, she followed him about so persistently; but his speech began to overflow with bitterness towards her. He said the cruellest things; then remembering them afterwards when alone, he blushed at his brutalities. But nothing he said ever altered her sweetness of temper or weakened the tenacity of her purpose. His rebuffs made her beautiful eyes run over with tears, but the harshest of them never elicited the least sign of resentment. There would have been something touching as well as comic in this dog-like forgiveness, which accepted everything as welcome at his hands, had he not been imbued with Mayne's conviction that it was all an admirable piece of acting. When for a moment he forgot the histrionic theory, then invariably there would come a chance word in her conversation which would fill him with cold rage. They would be talking of books, travels, sport, what not, and she would drop a reference to this man or to that. So-and-so had taken her to Bullier's, she had learned skating with this other. She was a capital shot, Hiram P. Ladd had taught her; and he got glimpses of long vistas of amourettes played in every State in America, and in every country of Europe, since the very beginning, when, as a mere child, elderly men, friends of her father's, had held her on their knee and fed her with sweetmeats and kisses. It was sickening to think of; it was pitiable. So much youth and beauty tarnished: the possibility for so much good thrown away. For if one could only blot out her record, forget it, accept her for what she chose to appear, a more endearing companion no man could desire.

V

It was a wet afternoon. Mayne had accompanied his wife and the Baroness into Hamelin. 'To take up a servant's character, and expostulate with a recalcitrant dress-maker,' he explained to Campbell, and wondered what women would do to fill up their days, were it not for the perennial villanies of dressmakers and domestic servants. He himself was going to look in at the English Club; wouldn't Campbell come too? There was a fourth seat in the carriage. But Campbell was in no social mood; he felt his temper going all to pieces; a quarter of an hour of Mrs Mayne's society would have brought on an explosion. He felt he must be alone; yet when he had read for half-an-hour in his room he wondered vaguely what Lulie was doing; he had not seen her since luncheon. She always gave him her society when he could very well dispense with it, but on a wet day like this, when a little conversation would be tolerable, of course she stayed away. Then there came down the long Rittersaal the tapping of high heels and a well-known knock at his door.

'Am I disturbing you?' she asked; and his mood was so capricious that, now she was standing there on his threshold, he thought he was annoyed at it. 'It's so dull,' she said, persuasively: 'Nannie's got a sick headache, and I daren't go downstairs, or the Baron will annex me to play Halma. He always wants to play Halma on wet days.'

'And what do you want to do?' said Campbell, leaning against the doorpost, and letting his eyes rest on the strange piquant face in its setting of red hair.

'To be with you, of course.'

'Well,' said he, coming out and closing the door, 'I'm at your service. What next?'

'What would you like to do? Shall I fetch over my pistols, and we'll practise with them? You've no notion how well I can shoot. We couldn't hurt anything here, could we?'

The Rittersaal is an immense room occupying all the space on the first floor that the hall and four drawing-rooms do on the floor below. Wooden pillars support the ceiling, and divide the room lengthwise into three parts. Down the centre are long tables, used for ceremonial banquets. Six windows look into the court-yard, and six out over the open country. The centre pane of each window is emblazoned with a Ritterhausen shield. The sills are broad and low, and cushioned in faded velvet. Between the windows hang family portraits, and a fine stone-sculptured sixteenth-century fireplace and over-mantel at one end of the *Saal* faces a magnificent black carved buffet at the other. Lulie, bundling up her duchess tea-gown over one arm, danced off down the long room in very unduchess-like fashion to fetch the case. It was a charming little box of cedar-wood and mother-o'-pearl, lined with violet velvet; and two tiny revolvers lay inside, hardly more than six inches long, with silver engraved handles.

'I won them in a bet,' she observed complacently, 'with the Hon. Billie Thornton. He's an Englishman, you know, the son of Lord Thornton. I knew him in Washington two years ago last fall. He bet I couldn't hit a three-cent piece at twenty feet, and I did. Aren't they perfectly sweet? Now, can't you contrive a target?'

Campbell went back to his room, drew out a rough diagram, and pasted it down on to a piece of stout card-board. Then this was fixed up by means of a penknife driven into the wood against one of the pillars, and Campbell, with his walking-stick laid down six successive times, measured off the distance required, and set a chalk mark across the floor. Lulie took the first shot. She held the little weapon out at arm's length – pulled the trigger. There was the sharp report, and when Campbell went up to examine results, he found she had only missed the very centre by half an inch.

Lulie was exultant. 'I don't seem to have got out of practice any,' she remarked. 'I'm so glad, for I used to be a very good shot. It was Hiram P. Ladd who taught me. He's the crack shot of Montana. What! you don't know Hiram P.? Why, I should have supposed every one must have heard of him. He had the next ranch to my Uncle

79

Samuel's, where I used to go summers, and he made me do an hour's pistol practice every morning after bathing. It was he who taught me swimming too – in the river.'

'Damnation,' said Campbell under his breath, then shot in his turn, and shot wide. Lulie made another bull's eye, and after that a white. She urged Campbell to continue, which he sullenly did, and again missed.

'You see I don't come up to your Hiram P. Ladd,' he remarked savagely, and after a few more shots on either side he put the pistol down, and walked over to the window. He stood with one foot on the cushioned seat, staring out at the rain, and pulling at his moustache moodily.

Lulie followed him, nestled up to him, lifted the hand that hung passive by his side, put it round her waist, and held it there. Campbell, lost in thought, let it remain so for a second: then remembered how she had doubtless done this very same thing with other men in this very room. All her apparently spontaneous movements, he told himself, were but the oft-used pieces in the game she played so skilfully.

'Let go,' he said, and flung himself down on the window-seat, looking up at her with darkening eyes.

She sat meekly in the other corner, and folded her offending hands in her lap.

'Do you know, your eyes are not a bit nice when you're cross;' she said, 'they seem to become quite black.'

He maintained a discouraging silence.

She looked over at him meditatively.

'I never cared a bit for Hiram P., if that's what you mean,' she remarked presently.

'Do you suppose I care a button if you did?'

'Then why did you leave off shooting, and why won't you talk to me?'

He vouchsafed no reply.

Lulie spent some moments wrapped in thought. Then she sighed deeply, and recommenced on a note of pensive regret:

'Ah, if I'd only met you sooner in life, I should be a very different girl.'

The freshness which her quaint, drawling enunciation lent to this time-dishonoured formula, made Campbell smile. Then remembering all its implications, his face set in frowns again.

Lulie continued her discourse. 'You see,' said she, 'I never had any one to teach me what was right. My mother died when I was quite a child, and my father has always let me do exactly as I pleased, so long as I didn't bother him. Then I've never had a home, but have always lived around in hotels and places; all winter in New York or Washington, and summers out at Longbranch or Saratoga. It's true we own a house in Detroit on Lafayette Avenue, that we reckon as home, but we don't ever go there. It's a bad sort of life for a girl, isn't it?' she questioned, pleadingly.

His mind was at work. The loose threads of his angers,

81

his irritations, his desires were knitting themselves together, weaving themselves into something overmastering and definite.

The young girl meanwhile was moving up towards him along the seat, for the effect which his sharpest rebuke produced on her never lasted more than four minutes. She now again possessed herself of his hand, and holding it between her own, began to caress it in child-like fashion, pulling the fingers apart and closing them again; spreading it, palm downwards on her lap, and laying her own little hand over it, to exemplify the differences between them. He let her be; he seemed unconscious of her proceedings.

'And then,' she continued, 'I've always known a lot of young fellows who've liked to take me round; and no one ever objected to my going with them, and so I went. And I liked it, and there wasn't any harm in it, just kissing and making believe, and nonsense. And I never really cared for one of them – I can see that now, when I compare them with you; when I compare what I felt for them, with what I feel for you. Oh, I do love you so much,' she said; 'don't you believe me?' She lifted his hand to her lips and covered it with kisses.

He pulled it roughly away, got up, walked to the table, came back again, stood looking at her with sombre eyes and dilating pupils.

'I do love you,' she repeated, rising and advancing towards him.

'For God's sake, drop that damned rot,' he cried with sudden fury. 'It wearies me, do you hear? it sickens me. Love, love, my God, what do you know about it? Why, if you really loved me, really loved any man – if you had any conception of what the passion of love is, how beautiful, how fine, how sacred – the mere idea that you could not come to your lover fresh, pure, untouched, as a young girl should – that you had been handled, fondled, and God knows what besides, by this man and the other – would fill you with such horror for yourself, with such supreme disgust – you would feel yourself so unworthy, so polluted . . . that . . . that . . . by God! you would take up that pistol there, and blow your brains out!'

Lulie seemed to find the idea quite entertaining. She picked the pistol up from where it lay in the window, examined it with her pretty head drooping on one side, looked at it critically, and then sent one of her long, red-brown caressing glances up towards him.

'And suppose I were to,' she asked lightly, 'would you believe me then?'

'Oh, . . . well . . . then, perhaps; if you showed sufficient decency to kill yourself, perhaps I might,' said he, with ironical laughter. His ebullition had relieved him; his nerves were calmed again. 'But nothing short of that would ever make me.'

With her little tragic air which seemed so like a smile disguised, she raised the weapon to the bosom of her gown. There came a sudden, sharp crack, a tiny smoke

83

film. She stood an instant swaying slightly, smiling certainly, distinctly outlined against the background of rain-washed window, of grey falling rain, the top of her head cutting in two the Ritterhausen escutcheon. Then all at once there was nothing at all between him and the window; he saw the coat-of-arms entire; but a motionless, inert heap of plush and lace, and fallen wine-red hair, lay at his feet upon the floor.

'Child, child, what have you done?' he cried with anguish, and kneeling beside her, lifted her up, and looked into her face.

When from a distance of time and place Campbell was at last able to look back with some degree of calmness on the catastrophe, the element which stung him most keenly was this: he could never convince himself that Lulie had really loved him after all. And the only two persons who had known them both, and the circumstances of the case, sufficiently well to have resolved his doubts one way or the other, held diametrically opposite views.

'Well, just listen, then, and I'll tell you how it was,' Miss Nannie Dodge had said to him impressively, the day before he left Schloss Altenau for ever, 'Lulie was tremendously, terribly in love with you. And when she found that you wouldn't care about her, she didn't want to live any more. As to the way in which it happened, you don't need to reproach yourself for that. She'd have done it, anyhow: if not then, why, later. But it's all the rest of your conduct to her that was so cruel. Your cold, complacent British unresponsiveness. I guess you'll never find another woman to love you as Lulie did. She was just the darlingest, the sweetest, the most loving girl in the world.'

Mayne, on the other hand, summed it up in this way: 'Of course, old chap, it's horrible to think of: horrible, horrible, horrible! I can't tell you how badly I feel about it. For she was a gorgeously beautiful creature. That red hair of hers! Good Lord! You won't come across such hair as that twice in a lifetime. But, believe me, she was only fooling with you. Once she had you in her hunting-noose, once her buccaneering instincts satisfied, and she'd have chucked you as she did all the rest. As to her death, I've got three theories – no, two – for the first is that she compassed it in a moment of genuine emotion, and that, I think, we may dismiss as quite untenable. The second is, that it arose from pure misadventure. You'd both been shooting, hadn't you? Well, she took up the pistol and pulled the trigger from mere mischief, and quite forgetting one barrel was still loaded. And the third is, it was just her histrionic sense of the fitness of things. The rôle she had played so long and so well now demanded a sensational finale in the centre of the stage. And it's the third theory I give the preference to. She was the most consummate little actress I ever saw.'

L'Education sentimentale

The Ring of Life

By Edmund Gosse

We trod the bleak ridge, to and fro,
    Grave forty, gay fourteen;
The yellow larks in Heaven's blue glow
    Like twinkling stars were seen,
And pink-flower'd larches, fring'd below,
    Were fabulously green.

And, as I watched my restless son
    Leap over gorse and briar,
And felt his golden nature run
    With April sap and fire,
Methought another madpate spun
    Beside another sire.

Sudden, the thirty years wing by,
    Shot, like a curtain's rings;
My father treads the ridge, and I
    The boy that leaps and flings;
While eyes that in the churchyard lie,
    Seem smiling tenderest things.

A Letter Home

By Arnold Bennett

I

Rain was falling – it had fallen steadily through the night – but the sky showed promise of fairer weather. As the first streaks of dawn appeared, the wind died away, and the young leaves on the trees were almost silent. The birds were insistently clamorous, vociferating times without number that it was a healthy spring morning and good to be alive.

A little, bedraggled crowd stood before the park gates, awaiting the hour named on the notice board when they would be admitted to such lodging and shelter as iron seats and overspreading branches might afford. A weary patient-eyed, dogged crowd – a dozen men, a boy of thirteen, and a couple of women, both past middle age – which had been gathering slowly since five o'clock. The boy appeared to be the least uncomfortable. His feet were bare, but he had slept well in an area in Grosvenor Place, and was not very damp yet. The women had nodded on many doorsteps, and were soaked. They stood apart from the men, who seemed unconscious of their existence. The men were exactly such as one would have expected to find there – beery and restless as to the eyes, quaintly shod, and with nondescript greenish clothes which for the most part bore traces of the yoke of the sandwich board. Only one amongst them was different.

He was young, and his cap, and manner of wearing it, gave sign of the sea. His face showed the rough outlines of his history. Yet it was a transparently honest face, very pale, but still boyish and fresh enough to make one wonder by what rapid descent he had reached his present level. Perhaps the receding chin, the heavy, pouting lower lip, and the ceaselessly twitching mouth offered a key to the problem.

'Say, Darkey,' he said.

'Well?'

'How much longer?'

'Can't ye see the clock? It's staring ye in the face.'

'No. Something queer's come over my eyes.'

Darkey was a short, sturdy man, who kept his head down and his hands deep in his pockets. The rain-drops clinging to the rim of an ancient hat fell every now and then into his grey beard, which presented a drowned appearance. He was a person of long and varied experience; he knew that queer feeling in the eyes, and his heart softened.

'Come, lean against the pillar,' he said, 'if you don't want to tumble. Three of brandy's what you want. There's four minutes to wait yet.'

With body flattened to the masonry, legs apart, and head thrown back, Darkey's companion felt more secure, and his mercurial spirits began to revive. He took off his cap, and brushing back his light brown curly hair with the hand which held it, he looked down at Darkey through half-closed eyes, the play of his features divided between a smile and a yawn. He had a lively sense of humour, and the irony of his situation was not lost on him. He took a grim, ferocious delight in calling up the might-have-beens and the 'fatuous ineffectual yesterdays' of life. There is a certain sardonic satisfaction to be gleaned from a frank recognition of the fact that you are the architect of your own misfortune. He felt that satisfaction, and laughed at Darkey, who was one of those who bleat about 'ill-luck' and 'victims of circumstance.'

'No doubt,' he would say, 'you're a very deserving fellow, Darkey, who's been treated badly. I'm not.' To have attained such wisdom at twenty-five is not to have lived altogether in vain.

A park-keeper presently arrived to unlock the gates, and the band of outcasts straggled indolently towards the nearest sheltered seats. Some went to sleep at once, in a sitting posture. Darkey produced a clay pipe, and, charging it with a few shreds of tobacco laboriously gathered from his waistcoat pocket, began to smoke. He was accustomed to this sort of thing, and with a pipe in his mouth could contrive to be moderately philosophical upon occasion. He looked curiously at his companion, who lay stretched at full length on another bench.

'I say, pal,' he remarked, 'I've known ye two days; ye've never told me yer name, and I don't ask ye to. But I see ye've not slep' in a park before.'

'You hit it, Darkey; but how?'

'Well, if the keeper catches ye lying down he'll be on to ye. Lying down's not allowed.'

The man raised himself on his elbow.

'Really now,' he said, 'that's interesting. But I think I'll give the keeper the opportunity of moving me. Why, it's quite fine, the sun's coming out and the sparrows are hopping round – cheeky little devils! I'm not sure that I don't feel jolly.'

'I wish I'd got the price of a pint about me,' sighed Darkey, and the other man dropped his head and appeared to sleep. Then Darkey dozed a little and heard in his waking sleep the heavy, crunching tread of an approaching park-keeper; he started up to warn his companion, but thought better of it, and closed his eyes again.

'Now then, there,' the park-keeper shouted to the man with the sailor hat, 'get up! This ain't a fourpenny doss, you know. No lying down.' A rough shake accompanied the words, and the man sat up.

'All right, my friend.' The keeper, who was a good-humoured man, passed on without further objurgation.

The face of the younger man had grown whiter.

'Look here, Darkey,' he said, 'I believe I'm done for.'

'Never say die.'

'No, just die without speaking.' His head fell forward and his eyes closed.

'At any rate, this is better than some deaths I've seen,' he began again with a strange accession of liveliness. 'Darkey, did I tell you the story of the five Japanese girls?'

'What, in Suez Bay?' said Darkey, who had heard many sea stories during the last two days, and recollected them but hazily.

'No, man. This was at Nagasaki. We were taking in a cargo of coal for Hong Kong. Hundreds of little Jap girls pass the coal from hand to hand over the ship's side in tiny baskets that hold about a plateful. In that way you can get 3000 tons aboard in two days.'

'Talking of platefuls reminds me of sausage and mash,' said Darkey.

'Don't interrupt. Well, five of these gay little dolls wanted to go to Hong Kong, and they arranged with the Chinese sailors to stow away; I believe their friends paid those cold-blooded fiends something to pass them down food on the voyage and give them an airing at nights. We had a particularly lively trip, battened everything down tight, and scarcely uncovered till we got into port.

Then I and another man found those five girls among the coal.'

'Dead, eh?'

'They'd simply torn themselves to pieces. Their bits of frock things were in strips, and they were scratched deep from top to toe. The Chinese had never troubled their heads about them at all, although they must have known it meant death. You may bet there was a row. The Japanese authorities make you search ship before sailing, now.'

'Well?'

'Well, I sha'n't die like that. That's all.'

He stretched himself out once more, and for ten minutes neither spoke. The park-keeper strolled up again.

'Get up, there!' he said shortly and gruffly.

'Up ye get, mate,' added Darkey, but the man on the bench did not stir. One look at his face sufficed to startle the keeper, and presently two policemen were wheeling an ambulance cart to the hospital. Darkey followed, gave such information as he could, and then went his own ways.

II

In the afternoon the patient regained full consciousness. His eyes wandered vacantly about the illimitable ward, with its rows of beds stretching away on either side of him. A woman with a white cap, a white apron, and white

wristbands bent over him, and he felt something grate-
fully warm passing down his throat. For just one second
he was happy. Then his memory returned, and the nurse
saw that he was crying. When he caught the nurse's eye
he ceased, and looked steadily at the distant ceiling.

'You're better?'

'Yes.' He tried to speak boldly, decisively, nonchalantly.
He was filled with a sense of physical shame, the shame
which bodily helplessness always experiences in the presence of arrogant, patronising health. He would have got
up and walked briskly away if he could. He hated to be
waited on, to be humoured, to be examined and the-
orised about. This woman would be wanting to feel his
pulse. She should not; he would turn cantankerous. No
doubt they had been saying to each other, 'And so young,
too! How sad!' Confound them.

'Have you any friends that you would like to send for?'

'No, none.'

The girl (she was only a girl) looked at him, and there
was that in her eye which overcame him.

'None at all?'

'Not that I want to see.'

'Are your parents alive?'

'My mother is, but she lives away in the North.'

'You've not seen her lately, perhaps?'

He did not reply, and the nurse spoke again, but her
voice sounded indistinct and far off.

When he awoke it was night. At the other end of the

ward was a long table covered with a white cloth, and on this table a lamp.

In the ring of light under the lamp was an open book, an inkstand, and a pen. A nurse (not *his* nurse) was standing by the table, her fingers idly drumming the cloth, and near her a man in evening dress. Perhaps a doctor. They were conversing in low tones. In the middle of the ward was an open stove, and the restless flames were reflected in all the brass knobs of the bedsteads and in some shining metal balls which hung from an unlighted chandelier. His part of the ward was almost in darkness. A confused, subdued murmur of little coughs, breathings, rustlings, was continually audible, and sometimes it rose above the conversation at the table. He noticed all these things. He became conscious, too, of a strangely familiar smell. What was it? Ah, yes! Acetic acid – his mother used it for her rheumatics.

Suddenly, magically, a great longing came over him. He must see his mother, or his brothers, or his little sister – some one who knew him, some one who *belonged* to him. He could have cried out in his desire. This one thought consumed all his faculties. If his mother could but walk in just now through that doorway! If only old Spot, even, could amble up to him, tongue out and tail furiously wagging! He tried to sit up, and he could not move! Then despair settled on him, and weighed him down. He closed his eyes.

The doctor and the nurse came slowly up the ward,

pausing here and there. They stopped before his bed, and he held his breath.

'Not roused up again, I suppose?'

'No.'

'Hm! He may flicker on for forty-eight hours. Not more.'

They went on, and with a sigh of relief he opened his eyes again. The doctor shook hands with the nurse, who returned to the table and sat down.

Death! The end of all this! Yes, it was coming. He felt it. His had been one of those wasted lives of which he used to read in books. How strange! Almost amusing! He was one of those sons who bring sorrow and shame into a family. Again, how strange! What a coincidence that he, just *he* and not the man in the next bed, should be one of those rare, legendary good-for-nothings who go recklessly to ruin. And yet, he was sure that he was not such a bad fellow after all. Only somehow he had been careless. Yes, careless, that was the word . . . nothing worse . . . As to death, he was indifferent. Remembering his father's death, he reflected that it was probably less disturbing to die oneself than to watch another pass.

He smelt the acetic acid once more, and his thoughts reverted to his mother. Poor mother! No, great mother! The grandeur of her life's struggle filled him with a sense of awe. Strange that until that moment he had never seen the heroic side of her humdrum, commonplace existence! He must write to her, now, at once, before it was too late.

His letter would trouble her, add another wrinkle to her face, but he must write; she must know that he had been thinking of her.

'Nurse,' he cried out, in a thin, weak voice.

'Ssh!' She was by his side directly, but not before he had lost consciousness again.

The following morning he managed with infinite labour to scrawl a few lines:

'Dear Mamma,

'You will be surprised but not glad to get this letter. I'm done for, and you will never see me again. I'm sorry for what I've done, and how I've treated you, but it's no use saying anything now. If Pater had only lived he might have kept me in order. But you were too kind, you know. You've had a hard struggle these last six years, and I hope Arthur and Dick will stand by you better than I did, now they are growing up. Give them my love, and kiss little Fannie for me.

'WILLIE.'

'Mrs Hancock—'

He got no further with the address.

III

By some strange turn of the wheel, Darkey gathered several shillings during the next day or two, and feeling both elated and benevolent, he called one afternoon at the hospital, 'just to inquire like.' They told him the man was dead.

'By the way, he left a letter without an address. Mrs Hancock – here it is.'

'That'll be his mother; he did tell me about her – lived at Endon, Staffordshire, he said. I'll see to it.'

They gave Darkey the letter.

'So his name's Hancock,' he soliloquised, when he got into the street. 'I knew a girl of that name – once. I'll go and have a pint of four half.'

At nine o'clock that night Darkey was still consuming four half, and relating certain adventures by sea which, he averred, had happened to himself. He was very drunk.

'Yes,' he said, 'and them five lil' gals was lying there without a stitch on 'em, dead as meat; 's'true as I'm 'ere. I've seen a thing or two in my time, I can tell ye.'

'Talking about these Anarchists—' said a man who appeared anxious to change the subject.

'An–kists,' Darkey interrupted. 'I tell ye what I'd do with that muck.' He stopped to light his pipe, looked in vain for a match, felt in his pockets, and pulled out a piece of paper – the letter.

'I tell you what I'd do. I'd—' He slowly and meditatively tore the letter in two, dropped one piece on the floor, thrust the other into a convenient gas jet, and applied it to the tobacco.

'I'd get 'em 'gether in a heap and I'd— Damn this pipe.' He picked up the other half of the letter, and relighted the pipe.

'After you, mate,' said a man sitting near, who was just biting the end from a cigar.

The Blessed

By W. B. Yeats

Cumhal the king, being angry and sad,
   Came by the woody way
To the cave, where Dathi the Blessed had gone,
   To hide from the troubled day.

Cumhal called out, bowing his head,
   Till Dathi came and stood,
With blinking eyes, at the cave's edge,
   Between the wind and the wood.

And Cumhal said, bending his knees,
   'I come by the windy way
To gather the half of your blessedness
   And learn the prayers that you say.

'I can bring you salmon out of the streams
   And heron out of the skies.'
But Dathi folded his hands and smiled
   With the secrets of God in his eyes.

And Cumhal saw like a drifting smoke
   All manner of blessedest souls,
Children and women and tonsured young men,
   And old men with croziers and stoles.

'And who is the blessedest,' Cumhal said,
  'Where all are comely and good?
Is it those that with golden thuribles
  Are singing about the wood?'

'My eyes are blinking,' Dathi said,
  'With the secrets of God half blind.
But I have found where the wind goes
  And follow the way of the wind;

'And blessedness goes where the wind goes
  And when it is gone we die;
And have seen the blessedest soul in the world,
  By a spilled wine-cup lie.

'O blessedness comes in the night and the day,
  And whither the wise heart knows;
And one has seen, in the redness of wine,
  The Incorruptible Rose:

'The Rose that must drop, out of sweet leaves,
  The heaviness of desire,
Until Time and the World have ebbed away
  In twilights of dew and fire!'

The Mysterious Rose Garden